Enid Blyton's

MAGICAL TALES

Games in Goblinland

and other stories

This is a Parragon Book

© Parragon 1997

13-17 Avonbridge Trading Estate,
Atlantic Road, Avonmouth, Bristol
Produced by The Templar Company plc,
Pippbrook Mill, London Road, Dorking,
Surrey RH4 1JE

Text copyright © Enid Blyton Ltd 1926-29

These stories were first published in Sunny Stories,
Teacher's Treasury, Two Years in the Infant School,
Read to Us, New Friends and Old and
The Daily Mail Annual.

Enid Blyton's signature mark is a registered
trademark of Enid Blyton Limited.

Edited by Caroline Repchuk and Dugald Steer

Designed by Mark Kingsley-Monks

Printed and bound in Italy

ISBN 0 7525 1707 4 (Hardback)
ISBN 0 7525 2317 1 (Paperback)

Enid Blyton's

Games in Goblinland

and other stories

Contents

Games in Goblinland

ALLAN loved playing games indoors on a rainy day. He had draughts, snap and beat-your-neighbour-out-of-doors. I expect you know how to play them all, don't you?

But nobody liked playing games with Allan because he always wanted to win – and if he didn't, he either cheated or flew into a temper and wouldn't play any more!

His father was angry with him. "You must learn to lose, as well as to win!" he often said to Allan. "You must never cheat, and as for flying into a temper and throwing the cards and the counters about – well! You ought to be ashamed of yourself!"

Now one day it was wet, and a friend of Allan's mother came to ask if Allan would like to bring his games to her house and play them with Michael, her little boy. So Allan took a basket with his draught-board and counters in, and his two packs of cards to play snap and beat-your-neighbour-out-of-doors.

He ran down a little path that went down the side of a field, and, as he ran, the box of counters upset and rolled out of the basket. Allan bent down to pick them up. He found all but one, and this last one he could not find!

He thought it must have gone into the thick hedge that grew by the side of the path, so he crawled into it – and then he had the surprise of his life!

In the shelter of the hedge sat three small goblins, playing a curious game with fans and balls that Allan had never seen before. He stared and stared – and they stared back.

"Come and play," said one of the goblins. He offered Allan a fan and two balls. The little boy took them in delight and sat down beside the goblins. This *was* an exciting adventure!

But he couldn't play the game, however much he tried – so he fetched his basket of games, and showed them to the goblins.

"We do not know how to play those games," they said.

"Oh, they are easy," said Allan, at once, delighted to think that if the goblins did not know how to play the games, he would easily win! "This game is called draughts. And this one is called snap. And this one, played with these cards, is called beat-your-neighbour-out-of-doors!"

He showed the goblins how to play draughts – and one of them began to play with him. But, you know, goblin brains are sharp – and the little fellow easily beat Allan! The little boy lost his temper – and what do you suppose he did? He picked up the draught-board and threw it hard at the surprised goblin!

There was a silence for a moment. Then the goblin stood up and frowned angrily.

"So that's how you play your game of draughts!" he said. "I suppose you play your games of snap and beat-your-neighbour-out-of-doors in the same way! Well! Come with us and we will show you how we play those

games in our country! We will
see if you like that!"

The three goblins caught hold
of the bad-tempered little boy
and pushed him through the
hedge to the other side – and to
Allan's enormous astonishment,
he saw that he was in a small
town of little hillocks, in each of
which lived a goblin. The three
goblins with Allan clapped their
hands and called out something.
At once the doors in the hillock-
houses flew open and out came
scores of small goblins just like
the others, all dressed in grey
suits and hats, and all with
pointed ears and feet.

"We want to teach this boy a few games," said one of the three goblins, with a grin. "It seems to us that he doesn't know how to play the games he has with him. First we would like to teach him how to play draughts!"

"Ho, ho, ho!" laughed all the goblins at once. "We will show him!" They stood in a ring and took hands. "Come into the middle!" they shouted to Allan. "We will show you how to play our game of draughts!"

Allan was pushed into the middle of the ring. Then the goblins danced round once, and sang a strange, chanting song

that went like this:
      "North wind blow!
      South wind too!
      East and West wind
      Where are YOU?"
Immediately there came the four winds, blowing hard from the north, south, east and west. They came right into the ring of dancing goblins, and began to blow poor Allan!

His cap flew off, and his coat flew open. His hair stood up straight, and there was a loud whistling in his ears. He could hardly stand upright, and he felt dreadfully cold.

"This is our game of draughts!"

shouted the goblins, in glee. "Isn't it draughty? Do you feel a draught? Do you think you will win? It's no use losing your temper in this game – because the winds won't let you! They do love a game of draughts!"

Allan became so out of breath with the blowing of the four winds, that he could not say a single word. He staggered about in the ring of goblins, puffing and blowing, trying to keep his coat on and feeling colder and colder!

As suddenly as they had come, the winds went. The goblins unlinked their hands and laughed at Allan, who sat down to get his breath. He felt giddy.

"Did you like our game of draughts?" asked the goblins. "Wasn't it fun? Now we'll show you how to play snap!"

They made a ring again, and put Allan in the middle. Then they began to chant another song:

"Here's a chap
Who likes to snap.
Play with him, pup,
And snap him UP!"

Then into the ring there ran a big puppy dog, full of fun and nonsense. When he saw Allan he ran at him and snapped playfully at the little boy's legs.

"Don't, don't!" shouted Allan. "Go away! I don't want to play with you, you nasty little puppy. Go away!"

He flapped his handkerchief at the puppy, and it woofed joyfully. It snapped at the handkerchief and tore it in half. Allan became very angry.

"Look what you've done!" he cried. "You've spoilt my handkerchief. GO AWAY!"

The goblins shrieked with laughter to see the puppy playing snap with Allan. The little boy took off his cap and tried to smack the puppy with it. But the little dog snapped at it eagerly, snatched it right out of Allan's hand and ran off round the ring with it!

"He's snapped the cap, he's snapped the cap!" yelled the goblins. "Oh, doesn't he play snap well? Do you like the way we play snap here, Allan?"

The puppy shook the cap and bit it hard. Then he ran at Allan again and began to snap at his coat. The small boy was almost in tears, for, although he could see that the puppy would not hurt him, he was very angry to have to play such a strange, silly game of snap!

The puppy jumped up and

snapped a button off Allan's
coat. The goblins cheered him
and then sent him out of the ring.
Allan picked up his torn
handkerchief and his bitten cap
and button.

"Well, the puppy won that
game!" said the goblins. "Now
for a game of beat-your-
neighbour-out-of-doors!"

They took Allan to a small
hillock-house and pushed him
inside. They shut the door. He
was left alone for a minute or
two, and then the door suddenly
burst open. In came a small
goblin pretending to be very
angry. He waved a stick at Allan

and shouted, "Get out of my house or I will beat you out!" Allan rushed out at once and the goblin chased after him. Seeing the next house with the door standing open, Allan rushed inside and banged the door. But, dear me, there was a goblin in there, and he had a stick too! He jumped up and shouted.

"Get out of my house or I will beat you out!" Allan gave a shout and rushed out again, with the goblin after him, waving his stick. In and out of the hillock-houses they rushed, and at last Allan ran into an open door again, for he could see there was no goblin inside. He banged the door and bolted it. Then he sat down to get his breath.

"They can't get me out of here!" he thought to himself. But he was mistaken – for there came a rumbling in the chimney – and down came a goblin, almost dropping on top of Allan, who had bent down to see what the noise was.

"Get out of my house or I will beat you out!" shouted the goblin gleefully, waving his stick. Allan unbolted the door in a hurry and rushed outside.

All the other goblins stood there, grinning and shouting in

great delight.

"Do you like the way we play beat-your-neighbour-out-of-doors?" they cried. "Shall we teach you another game? We have a fine one called put-me-in-the-coal-hole!"

Allan thought that didn't sound at all a nice game, so he shook his head.

"No, thank you," he said. "Please let me go to my friend's. He is expecting me. I am sorry I lost my temper when I played draughts with you in the hedge. I like my way of playing our games best. I don't like yours at all."

"Well, if you had played your

game properly without losing your temper, we wouldn't have shown you how we could play!" said one of the goblins. "You can go on your way. We don't expect to ever see you here again – unless you forget how to play properly, and want to come and be taught by us!"

"No, I don't, thank you," said Allan. "Goodbye."

Allan went to the thick hedge that grew behind the little town of hillock-houses, and squeezed his way through it. And on the other side was the field he knew so well – and his basket of games lying on the path!

Allan picked up the basket and set off to Michael's house. He was soon there, and Michael opened the door for him. "What a long time you have been!" he said. "Whatever have you been doing? Did you get lost?"

"No – not exactly lost," said Allan, and he wouldn't say any more, for he was too ashamed to tell Michael all that had happened to him.

"Come along to the playroom and we will play our games there," said Michael. "We'll play draughts first." So up they went, and set out the board on the playroom table. They put out the counters and began the game.

Michael was cleverer than Allan at the game, and soon took all his men – but do you suppose Allan cheated or lost his temper? No – not a bit of it! He said "You've won, Michael. Now let's play snap."

So they got out the snap cards, and soon they were snapping away, taking each other's pile of cards. Allan thought of the way the goblins played snap with the puppy dog, and he couldn't help thinking that his and Michael's way was very much nicer!

"SNAP!" said Michael suddenly, whilst Allan was

thinking about the goblins and forgetting to look at the cards. Oh! Michael had snapped all his pile of cards – and had won!

"It isn't fair," said Allan, "because I was just thinking about..."

And just as he spoke he thought he heard a little sound of a goblin chuckling away to himself. He looked round quickly. No – there wasn't a goblin to be seen.

"It's all right," said Allan. "It's quite fair. I should have been looking at the game."

They began to play beat-your-neighbour-out-of-doors, and

would you believe it, Michael
seemed to have all the kings,
queens and aces in the pack – so
it wasn't very long before he had
beaten Allan again. But this time
the little boy was not going to
say a word about the win not
being fair – nor was he going to
lose his temper!

"It's your game again!" he said
to Michael. "Jolly good!"

And he thought he heard a
whisper somewhere: "Jolly good,
Allan! Well done!" But though
he looked all round again, there
was nobody there at all.

Allan plays games as they
should be played now – no

cheating, no grumbling, no losing of tempers. And one day he is going to squeeze through that thick hedge and tell those goblins something. He wants to say, "Thank you for teaching me all you did! I'll never forget it."

Won't they be surprised?

The Red and Yellow Hoop

JOHN had seen a ship in the toy shop window. It was a fine ship with a big white sail and it was called *The Sea Gull*. John badly wanted to buy it.

He emptied out his money-box. The ship cost three pounds and when he counted out his money he had just enough.

"Mummy, may I spend my money on a ship?" he asked. "I've got just enough. I've been saving for a long time."

"Yes, dear, if you like," said his mother. "Take Ann with you."

Ann was John's little sister. He was very fond of her, so he went to fetch her.

"Come along, Ann," he said.
"I'm going to buy a ship at the
toy shop. You can come with me,
if you'd like to."

So off they went, running down
the street, but just as they
reached the toy shop, Ann fell
over and cut her knee. She was
frightened and began to cry. John
felt sorry for her and bandaged
up her knee with his
handkerchief.

"Don't cry, Ann," he said.
"Your knee will soon get better.
Look! My handkerchief is
wrapped round it."

But Ann wouldn't stop crying.
She sobbed and sobbed and

wanted her mother. John really didn't know what to do.

"Oh, Ann, please stop crying!" he begged. "Listen! I'll buy you something at the toy shop if you like – but please stop crying!"

"Will you really buy me something?" she asked. "I thought you only had enough money for your ship."

"Never mind," said John. "I can save up again for the ship. I'll buy you something nice to make up for hurting your knee."

It was very kind of John. He did badly want his ship, and he knew quite well that if he bought a toy for Ann he wouldn't have enough money to buy his ship as well. But he was very fond of his little sister and he wanted to comfort her.

The two of them went into the shop and Ann looked round. She didn't know what to choose. Should it be a doll? Or a book? Or a toy train?

"Have you seen these lovely new hoops?" asked the shopkeeper, showing the little girl a heap of brightly coloured hoops. "Look, they are all painted different colours and they do look pretty when you bowl them round and round. The sticks are painted in all sorts of pretty colours, too."

"Oh, yes, I'd like a hoop!" said
Ann, pleased. "I'll have a red
and yellow one, please. A nice
big one, because I can run fast."

"How much are they?" asked
John, feeling in his pocket for the
money he had brought, and
trying very hard not to look at
the ship in the window.

"Three pounds, hoop and stick
together," said the shopkeeper.
So John paid him the money and
he and Ann left the shop
together. Ann was very happy. It
really was a beautiful hoop, and
she soon forgot about her hurt
knee as she bowled her hoop

along the road.

As they went along, they passed a river – and suddenly John heard a shout.

"Listen!" he said to Ann. "Was that a shout for help? Oh, I wonder if anyone has fallen into the river! Come quickly, Ann, and see!"

The two children rushed down to the riverside and looked in. They saw a little girl struggling in the water by herself. She had fallen in and couldn't get out. John couldn't swim, and the water was too deep for him to wade through. Whatever should he do? There was no one near to help. He must do something, or the little girl might drown.

Then a splendid idea came into his head. He called to Ann, who was looking very frightened.

"Give me your new hoop, Ann! I believe if I hold it out to that little girl she can just reach it. Then together we can pull her to the bank!"

In a trice Ann held out her
hoop to John and he ran to the
little girl. He caught hold of a
tree nearby and then, leaning as
far as he could over the water, he
held out the brightly coloured
hoop to the small girl.

"Catch hold!" he shouted.
"Catch hold!"

The hoop just reached her!
She put out her hands and
caught hold of it, pulling hard.
John was nearly dragged into the
water, too, but he held tightly to
the tree, and Ann held him
firmly round the waist.

"Hold tight!" shouted John,

and the little girl in the water clung tightly to the hoop. Then John pulled hard and gradually he managed to drag the child towards the bank. The hoop stretched out of shape with the weight and, just as John put out his hand and dragged the little girl to safety, it snapped in half! But the girl was safe, and she climbed out quickly.

"Oh, thank you, thank you!" she cried. "It was a good idea to use your hoop like that. I'm so sorry it's broken. I'll ask my Daddy to buy you a new one."

"That's all right," said John. "You'd better come home and

get dry. We live quite near here. My Mummy will dry you and give you some of Ann's clothes to wear."

So off they all went and soon she was being dried in front of the fire and John had been sent to tell the little girl's mother where she was.

Her mother and father came running to see if she was alright – and when they heard the story of the hoop, they were so grateful to Ann and John.

"You must come to tea tomorrow with Lucy," they said. "We will have a little party to show you how glad we are that you have saved our little girl."

The party was perfectly lovely – and, at the end of it, Lucy's mother brought out two big parcels, one for Ann and one for John. And what do you think was inside them?

Ann had another hoop, just like the one that had broken and, as for John, there was a wonderful sailing ship, far better than the one he had seen in the shop window! Wasn't he lucky!

"Well, you deserve it, John," said his mother when he got home. "You gave up your money to buy Ann a hoop when she fell down – and your kind deed has brought you something far better than the ship you were going to buy. I'm proud of you! You really do deserve your good luck."

Goldie, the Cat Who Said Thank You

"JEAN!" called Mummy. "I want you to go on an errand for me!"

"Where to?" asked Jean, running up.

"To Mrs Hunt's at Home Farm," said Mummy. "Fetch me six new-laid eggs, darling. The doctor says Daddy must have lots of them to make him better."

"All right," said Jean, and fetched her little egg basket. "I won't be long, Mummy."

Off she went, over the fields and across the little brown stream to Home Farm.

Mrs Hunt was feeding her chickens when Jean got to the

farm. She smiled at the little girl.

"Good morning, my dear," she said. "Do you want some of my nice eggs?"

"Yes, I would like six eggs, please." answered Jean. "Where's Philip?"

"Philip's round at the Big Barn," said Mrs Hunt. "He's got some fine kittens there, if you'd like to see them!"

"Yes, I should!" said Jean. "I'll go now."

She ran round to the Big Barn and went in. There she saw Philip, Mrs Hunt's son, bending over a litter of kittens lying in some hay.

"Hello, Jean!" he said. "Come and look at these! Two of them are real beauties!"

Jean bent over the kittens. Tibs, the mother cat, washed herself calmly and took no notice – she knew Philip and Jean would do no harm.

"They haven't got their eyes open yet," said Philip. "Aren't these two sweet? Their hair is long and silky already. They ought to be fine cats."

"But why don't you like the little third one?" asked Jean. "He looks quite a dear."

"What! That ugly little sandy fellow!" said Philip scornfully.

"He's not worth keeping!"

"But he can't help being that colour!" said Jean. "What are you going to do with him?"

"I'll have to drown him," answered Philip. "Mother will only let me keep two."

"Oh, poor wee thing!" cried Jean. "What a shame, just because he's not got long silky hair, like the others! Please don't drown him, Philip!"

"Well, you have him, then," said Philip. "You haven't got a cat, have you?"

"No, I haven't. Oh, I wonder if Mummy would let me have him?" cried Jean, jumping up.

"I'll go and ask her about it this very minute!"

She ran to Mrs Hunt and took the eggs. Then, going as fast as she dared, for she was afraid of breaking the precious eggs, she hurried home again.

"Mummy!" she called. "Here are the eggs. And oh, Mummy! Philip's got three kittens, and he's only allowed to keep two. The other will be drowned if I don't have it! Can I have it, Mummy? Oh, please can I?"

"Oh, Jean dear!" said Mummy. "I really don't think you can! I simply haven't any money at all to spare to pay for cat's milk!

Since Daddy's been ill, I haven't known how to manage!"

"Oh, Mummy! How much does cat's milk cost?" asked Jean. "Could I have the kitten if I give you the three pounds that Great Aunt Jane gives me every Saturday for running her errands for her?"

Mummy looked at Jean and thought for a moment.

"Do you want that kitten very badly?" she asked, smiling. "Is it worth as much as three pounds a week to you?"

"Oh yes!" answered Jean. "Don't let it be drowned, Mummy, please!"

"Well, you may have it," said Mummy. "You can pay me two pounds every Saturday, and keep the other one yourself."

"You darling!" squeaked Jean, and hugged Mummy as hard as ever she could. "Thank you."

"Well, you can go and tell Philip," said Mummy. "And you can fetch the kitten when it's old enough to leave its mother."

Jean ran off, feeling most excited, and told Philip what she was going to do.

"All right," he said. "It's a good thing for that kitten you came along when you did! I hope that it will be a grateful kitten and will say thank you!"

"Don't be silly, Philip," said Jean. "Cat's don't know how to say thank you."

In a few weeks Jean fetched the kitten to her own home. It was a little tabby, thin and not very pretty, but Jean didn't mind about that at all.

"You're certainly worth two pounds a week," she said, hugging the kitten to her. "And I'm going to spend my extra pound on a lovely piece of red ribbon for you."

The kitten loved Jean. It followed her about all over the place, and purred whenever it saw her. It played all sorts of tricks on her, and jumped at her feet as if they were a couple of scampering mice.

Jean loved the kitten, and when the little boy next door laughed at it, and called it "an ugly, common little tabby," she told him he was horrid.

"You shouldn't say that in front of the kitty," she scolded. "It will make him miserable!"

"Fiddlesticks! Kittens haven't any sense, as everyone knows!" laughed the boy.

"This one has!" said Jean, and took her kitten indoors without saying another word.

She couldn't think what to call him at first. Then, because he had fine golden whiskers, she called him Goldie.

He seemed to like his name very much, and always came scampering to Jean when she called him, wherever he happened to be.

"He's not at all a bad little kitten," said Mummy one day. "He's growing a lovely strong, smooth coat, Jean. He may be quite a nice cat, after all!"

"Of course he will!" said Jean. "I believe he will be beautiful, Mummy!"

"Oh, no dear, not beautiful,"

said Mummy. "He's only just a very ordinary tabby, you know!'

One day Great Aunt Jane asked Jean what she did with the money she got every week for running her errands on Saturday.

"I give Mummy two pounds of it to help pay for Goldie's milk," said Jean. "The other pound I spend on all sorts of things."

"Who's Goldie?" asked Great Aunt Jane.

"He's my own cat," said Jean. "He's a perfect darling."

She told Great Aunt Jane all about how she came to have him.

"Dear me! That's very interesting!" said Great Aunt

Jane. "I'm very fond of cats. I used to keep some beauties. You must bring your Goldie and let me see him next Saturday."

"Perhaps you won't think he's very beautiful," said Jean. "Nobody seems to think much of him, except me."

"Well, bring him, and I'll tell you exactly what I think," said Great Aunt with a smile.

So the next Saturday Jean carried Goldie all the way to Great Aunt Jane's. He had grown into a big cat, and his tail was very long. His eyes were amber green, and his whiskers were still very golden. He was heavy, but Jean didn't dare to put him down, just in case he ran away and got lost.

"Good morning, Aunt Jane," she panted, when she reached her Great Aunt's house at last. "I'm sorry I'm late, but Goldie was so heavy."

"So that's Goldie, is it?" said Aunt Jane, taking him from Jean. She stroked him and he purred loudly. Then she gave him a saucer of creamy milk, and watched him while he drank it.

"What do you think of him?" asked Jean, anxiously.

"Well, my dear, he's a real beauty!" said Aunt Jane. "You

must surely have taken great care of him to make him so sturdy and sleek!"

"Oh, do you really think he's beautiful?" asked Jean in delight.

"Do you know what he is?" asked Aunt Jane suddenly. "He's a golden tabby, and one of the finest I ever saw! I had two once, but they weren't nearly as lovely as your Goldie!"

Jean could hardly believe her ears. She suddenly hugged Aunt Jane, then she hugged Goldie, and then she hugged Aunt Jane once more.

"Bless the child!" said Aunt Jane. "She thinks I'm a cat too, to have all the breath squeezed out of me! Now I've got an idea, Jean. Listen!"

"What?" asked Jean, breathlessly.

"There's a cat show to be held here in a month's time," said Great Aunt. "We'll enter your Goldie in the Golden Tabby class, and see if wins a prize!"

"Oh! Oh! Do let's!" squeaked Jean in delight, hugging her Great Aunt again.

"Jean! Do let me breathe!" said Aunt Jane. "Well, if we do that you must keep Goldie very spick and span all month and brush him every day. You must see that he's fed well too. I will give you some money every week for him, so that Mummy won't be worried."

"You are a perfect dear," said Jean, hugging Goldie, instead of Aunt Jane.

So it was all arranged. Aunt Jane wrote to the Cat Show people and entered Goldie in the Golden Tabby class.

One day she gave Jean a big green ticket which had Goldie's name on it.

"Here you are," she said. "Next Saturday bring your Goldie here, and we'll put his cat show ticket on him. Then we'll all go to the show, and see what happens!"

Jean was so excited. She brushed Goldie every day, and fed him well and regularly. Mummy got quite excited too, when she heard about it all.

At last the cat show day came.

Mummy and Great Aunt Jane, Goldie and Jean, all went into the Town Hall, and found the place where Goldie was to sit that day.

Jean was so excited. Her knees kept shaking, so that she felt everyone must wonder what the matter with her legs was. When the Judges came round to look at

Goldie, she could hardly breathe.

And what do you think?

Goldie won the very first prize of all in the Golden Tabbies!

"He's a most beautifully shaped cat!" said one of the Judges. "And his colouring is lovely. Everything about him matches – his coat, his eyes, and his whiskers! Here's the first prize label, little girl. Hang it up by him!"

Jean couldn't say a word. She took the label, and hung it up for everyone to see. Mummy and Great Aunt Jane were pleased.

"I told you so. I told you so!" said Great Aunt, banging the floor with her stick.

And when Jean went to get Goldie's prize, she found it was twenty five pounds! She took Goldie up with her to get it, and everyone began to clap loudly.

But what Jean liked very nearly the best of all was when she carried Goldie over to Philip that evening.

"My word! What on earth is that label Goldie's got?" exclaimed Philip. "First prize! I say, Jean, how lovely!"

"Isn't it glorious?" said Jean, hugging Goldie, while he purred as loudly as a tiger. "And, oh Philip! This is his way of saying thank you for having saved him from drowning!"

And Goldie purred more loudly than ever, for Jean was quite right. He *had* meant to say thank you!

The One-Eyed Rabbit

THERE was once a toy rabbit who had two beautiful blue glass eyes. He could see very well indeed with them, and so it was a dreadful shock to him when he lost one.

They were stuck very tightly on to his head, not sewn on like the teddy bear's. Sometimes the teddy bear's eyes came loose and then they were wobbly, and everyone would laugh at him until somebody remembered to sew them back on his head properly again.

The rabbit was soft and cuddly, and he had a white tail at the back, and a beautiful pink ribbon tied round his neck. He was fluffy, jolly, kindly and very popular. He was always being asked out to parties by the pixies who lived in the daffodil bed below the playroom window. He used to ask the curly-haired doll to iron out his pink ribbon for him whenever he went out. He did so very much like to be neat and pretty.

Well, one day a dreadful thing happened. Janet took the rabbit, the curly-haired doll, and the teddy bear out into the garden with her – but when she came in again, she had forgotten all about the rabbit.

She put the curly-haired doll into her cot, and popped the teddy bear into his corner of the toy cupboard. The bear put his head out of the toy cupboard as soon as the little girl had gone out of the room, and called to the doll.

"I say, Curly-haired Doll, has the rabbit been left out in the garden?"

"Yes – isn't it dreadful!" said the doll, sitting up in her cot. "What are we going to do? Could you go and get him, do you think? He'll never, ever manage to find his way back to the playroom by himself."

"I'll have to wait till night-time," said the bear. "Somebody might see me if I go running out into the garden now."

So when night came, the bear slipped out of the window, climbed down the apple tree outside, and ran to the garden seat where Janet had played with him and the doll and the rabbit that morning. It was pouring with rain, and the bear was really very worried about the rabbit.

The rabbit was sitting on the seat feeling miserable, wet, and cold. He didn't like to jump down by himself because the seat was rather high. He was so pleased to see the bear.

"Oh, you are so nice to come and fetch me," said the rabbit joyfully. "Could you help me to get down from this high seat at all, Teddy?"

"Of course," said the bear, and he held out a plump, brown paw. The rabbit jumped, and landed on the grass. He rolled over, but he didn't hurt himself at all. Then, taking the bear's paw, he hurried up the wet garden to the apple tree, climbed to the window, and was soon safely inside the playroom being petted and fussed by all the toys.

And then, as he sat drying

himself by the fire, the curly-haired doll noticed a dreadful thing. The rabbit had only one eye! His left eye wasn't there!

"Oh, Rabbit!" she squealed in alarm. "Where's your left eye? It's come off! Did you know?"

The rabbit put up his paw and was dreadfully upset when he found that he only had one eye.

"I thought I couldn't see very well," he said. "The rain must have wetted it, and it came unstuck and fell off. Oh dear, oh dear – how awful!"

The bear at once climbed out of the window and went to look for the lost eye in the garden.

But he couldn't find it at all –
which wasn't very surprising,
because a worm had already
found it and taken it down his
hole. So the poor bear came back
without the eye.

The rabbit sat by the fire
miserably and wept big tears out
of his one eye.

"I look dreadful," he said. "I
shall never go out to parties
anymore. I shall never go out to
tea. No one will want a horrid
one-eyed rabbit. I shan't even go
for a walk again. And I don't
expect that Janet will love me
any more, now I've only got one
eye left."

"Don't be so silly, Rabbit," said everyone, but the rabbit just wouldn't be comforted. He wept and wept and wept.

Then the teddy bear had a marvellous idea. He jumped up and ran to the toy cupboard. He came back with Janet's new box of glass marbles. They were beautiful and she was very proud of them.

"Look, Rabbit," he said. "We may be able to find a nice blue glass marble that matches your right eye – and if we manage to saw it in half, we can stick it onto your head. Then you will have two eyes again and you can be happy once again!"

"But whatever will Janet say when she finds one of her marbles has been cut in half?" asked the rabbit.

"Well, as she was careless enough to leave you out in the rain, she deserves to lose half a marble," said the bear. And all the toys nodded and said he was absolutely right.

They soon found a marble that was exactly the right shade of blue. They had to call in one of the pixies to saw it in half, because none of the toys knew how to, and it needed a little magic to saw neatly through the glass of the marble.

The bear put one half back into the box of marbles. Then he found a tube of glue and squeezed some on to the flat side of the half-marble. Then he cleverly pressed it into the right place on the rabbit's head.

"Hold your new glass eye in place till it's stuck," he told the rabbit. So the rabbit held it there, and then, when it was properly stuck, he took his paw away – and there he was with two lovely blue eyes again.

"Oh, you look even nicer than before!" cried all the toys in delight. "Are you sure you can see all right, Rabbit?"

"Yes – it's a fine eye," said the rabbit joyfully, gazing all round the playroom with it. "In fact it's much better than my other one. Thank you, Teddy, for being so very clever."

He looked fine, though the marble eye was just a bit bigger than his other eye. But nobody minded that, and as for the rabbit, he never even knew it. He was so pleased and happy that he did a little rabbit dance all round the playroom and back again, and all the toys sat and clapped him and cheered.

What will Janet say when she

finds that one of her lovely marbles is cut in half? Do you think she will guess what has happened when she sees her rabbit's odd eye?

The
Disobedient
Doll

THE silly sailor doll never did as he was told. He was the silliest, most disobedient toy in the playroom. He just didn't care for anybody!

The big teddy bear was head of the playroom, and all the toys except the sailor doll took notice of what he said, and were careful to obey him. But the sailor doll only laughed at him!

"Never, ever play with matches," said the teddy bear. "They are very, very dangerous." So nobody did – except the silly sailor doll! He found a match-box and struck every single match in it. He even set fire to a piece of jigsaw and burnt it all up. It was lucky nothing else caught fire.

The bear was very angry.

"Now the children won't be able to make the picture which that bit of jigsaw belongs to," said the bear. "You are very naughty, Sailor Doll, and very, very silly."

Another time the bear saw that some fireworks in a box had been put into the toy-cupboard, ready for a party.

"You must never play with these," he said. "They could go off, and you would hurt yourself or someone else very badly!"

Well, of course, you can guess that the silly sailor doll at once got the box, opened it, and took out a firework. There were no more matches to light it with and so he threw it at the wall. It went BANG! threw out some silver sparks all over the red-haired doll, burned her hair, and then landed on the teddy bear. The sailor doll laughed till he cried at the poor burnt doll, which really was horrible of him.

The bear chased him all round the nursery, but he couldn't catch the bad sailor doll because he climbed up on to the window-sill. The big teddy bear was too fat to climb all the way up there.

"You wait!" he said to the sailor doll. "One of these days you'll get a shock, Sailor Doll, and you'll deserve to!"

"And one of these days you'll get a hundred," laughed the silly sailor doll. "You got a fine one tonight, didn't you, Teddy?"

"Don't take any notice of him," said the rabbit. "All he wants is to be noticed. Leave him alone and then maybe he will decide to become better."

Well, it was quite true – the silly sailor doll hated not to be looked at and spoken to. He was very vain and he loved to shock people. He tried all he could to make the toys notice him, but they just turned their heads away and wouldn't look at him at all.

Then a new toy came to the nursery. It was a blue aeroplane. It belonged to Billy. The sailor doll was most interested in it, for he thought it must be wonderful to fly in the air like a bird.

The aeroplane flew swiftly round the nursery and Billy was very pleased with it. He showed it to his sister, Shirley. "Look," he said, "if you want to make it fly, you wind this long elastic round and round and round underneath the aeroplane. Then

you hold it up like this – let it go
– and the elastic unwinds quickly
and sends the plane flying
through the air. Isn't it clever?"

All the toys thought the
aeroplane was marvellous,
especially the sailor doll. That
night they all stood round the
blue plane and looked at it.

"It would be quite easy to fly
it," said the rabbit. "Just wind up
the elastic and off it goes."

"Nobody is to fly this
aeroplane," said the teddy bear
at once. "We might break it. It
looked easy when we saw Billy
doing it, but it might not be so
easy if we tried."

"Very well, Teddy," said the toys. "We won't fly it."

Only the sailor doll didn't promise. He just longed and longed to fly the aeroplane – and what was more, he longed to go with it!

So whatever do you think he did? He went to the doll's swing in the corner and took away the little seat with ropes! The rabbit saw him and told the teddy bear.

"Oh, don't take any notice of him," said the bear crossly. "He just wants some attention. He can't get into any mischief with the swing."

But the sailor doll could! He

tied the ropes of the swing seat to the underneath of the aeroplane. That was to be his seat, you see, when the aeroplane flew off. It would take the swing seat with it, and the sailor doll thought he would have a wonderful time flying round the nursery.

Then the sailor doll wound up the elastic, pulling very tightly indeed. None of the toys looked to see what he was doing. They obeyed the bear and took no notice of him at all.

Whirrrr-rrr-rrr-rrr! The aeroplane flew off into the air! Whirrr-rrr-rrr! It flew all round the nursery, and the sailor doll flew too, sitting in the little toy swing seat below. My word, what excitement! Whirr-rrr-rrr! The aeroplane flew right out of the window and into the blackness of the night!

"I say! We'll have to take a bit of notice now!" cried the rabbit. "The aeroplane has gone out of the window, and that monkey of a sailor doll has gone with it!"

CRASH! A big noise came in at the window, and the toys went pale and looked at one another in fright. The aeroplane had crashed!

"I suppose we shall just have to

go and look for it," said the teddy bear. So they helped teddy up on to the window-sill and they all climbed out of the window and hurried to find the aeroplane. The teddy bear was clever enough to take Billy's little torch with him, and he switched it on and looked all round.

"There's the aeroplane – look!" cried the rabbit. And sure enough, there it was on the ground, upside down! But there was no sign of the sailor doll anywhere!

The toys turned the plane the right way up. It didn't seem to be hurt at all. It had bumped into a holly bush and had fallen to the ground. The toys thought they could get it back into the nursery all right. But they couldn't untie the knots that tied the swing seat to the aeroplane. So they had to leave them but they couldn't help wondering what Billy and Shirley would say the next day, when they saw it!

Then they heard somebody crying, and the bear flashed his torch about to find the sailor doll. Where do you think he was? Up in the prickly holly bush, hanging by his trousers! He had fallen out when the aeroplane had flown into the tree and the prickles were holding him tightly.

"Help me! Help me!" wept the sailor doll. "Get me down! The holly is pricking me dreadfully!"

"We can't possibly get you down," said the bear. "Who do you suppose is going to climb a prickly holly bush to rescue a bad doll like you? You'll have to stay there. I'm sorry, but we just can't help it!"

They all went back to the nursery, carrying the aeroplane. They managed to get it in at the window. The sailor doll was left outside.

It began to rain and he got wet. The rain trickled down his neck. The holly pricked him. He felt very cold and damp. He was frightened, because a spider ran over him, and asked if she could spin her web from his nose right down to his toes!

"Why have I been so bad? Why did I disobey the bear?" he sobbed. "This really is dreadful! A-tish-oo! Now I'm getting a horrible cold! Oh, if only I could get back into the nice, warm playroom, I would never, ever be disobedient again!"

The rain stopped. The wind began to blow. How it blew! The

holly bush shook from top to bottom. It stuck its prickles into the doll harder than ever.

The wind blew so hard that the doll was afraid of falling. He tried to take hold of the holly leaves to stop himself from falling, but they were so prickly that he had to let go. And down he went to the ground! The prickles tore his clothes as he went. The ground bumped him hard. At last he picked himself up, and sneezing and snuffling, he limped back to the nursery. He climbed in at the window.

"Ah! Here's the bold adventurer back again!" said the

teddy bear. "I hope you enjoyed yourself, Sailor Doll."

"Well I didn't," sniffed the doll. "A-tish-oo! A-tish-oo! I'm wet. I'm cold. I'm torn. I'm prickled. Whatever shall I do?"

"Get into the doll's cot and keep warm then," said the rabbit, who had a kind heart. "You do look dreadful, Sailor Doll! I shouldn't be at all surprised if you get thrown into the dustbin tomorrow!"

"Ohhhhh!" squealed the sailor doll in fright. He crept into the doll's cot and drew the bedclothes round him. He soon fell asleep, though he even sneezed in his sleep!

Next day Billy and Shirley found the swing seat tied under the aeroplane and they guessed one of the toys had been for a flight. When they found the wet, torn sailor doll, they knew at once that it was he who had taken the aeroplane to fly.

Shirley gave him a good telling off. "You might have broken the aeroplane," she said. "Teddy! You are the head of the playroom. Just see that it doesn't happen again!"

But he doesn't need to bother, for the sailor doll has had such a fright that he says he'll never be

naughty or silly again. He will
never play with matches or
fireworks or anything like that
and he still can't help sneezing
every time he thinks of that
horrible, cold, wet night!

Catch Him Quick

"WOULD you like to see my pet white mice, Ian?" asked Alice, when Ian came to tea one afternoon.

"Oooh, yes," said Ian. "I'm not allowed to keep pet mice – but I wish I was. I do like them."

"I'll get mine. They're called Bubble and Squeak," said Alice. "I'll bring them up to my playroom. You wait here."

She had soon brought the two white mice in their little cage. They were so tame that they ran all over Alice and Ian, and twitched their little pink noses as they sniffed about here, there and everywhere.

"Oh, I do wish I had two lovely little mice like these," said Ian. "I really do."

After a while Mummy called out that their tea was ready. "We'd better put the mice back into their cage and go." said Alice. "We'll play with them again afterwards."

The two mice were quickly put back into their cage. Alice swung the little door shut and latched it. Then they went downstairs to have their tea.

But Alice hadn't latched the door properly. It fell open – and the mice were easily able to get out! Squeak didn't want to get out. She was always afraid of cats when the playroom was empty. But Bubble was much bolder. He ran out at once.

The toys had been very interested, watching the two mice while the children were playing with them. Now, when Bubble came running out, the sailor doll sat up in a hurry.

"Catch him, quick! He's escaping! The children will be very upset if they find him gone."

"Catch me if you can!" said Bubble and scampered about the playroom floor. The sailor doll chased him. The teddy bear tried to head him off. The curly-haired doll tried to trap the naughty mouse in a corner.

But the mouse was much too clever to be caught. He ran here, he ran there – he laughed at the toys, and not one of them could manage to catch him.

"There he goes. Catch him, quick!" shouted the sailor doll again, as the mouse rushed out from under the couch.

Off they all went, after the mouse. Just as they thought they had finally got him, he slipped away again.

"Can't catch me! Can't catch me!" he called.

The sailor doll stopped, out of

breath. He thought hard for a minute. Then a big grin spread over his handsome face.

He whispered to the bear. "I've got an idea. I'm going to hide behind the curtain where no one will see me. And I'm going to make a noise like a cat!"

"Ooooh, Sailor Doll! That is a good idea!" said the bear. "That will give the naughty little mouse such a fright. He will go rushing back to his cage at once!"

The sailor doll slipped quietly behind the curtain. Then he began to mew.

"Meeow-ee-ow-ee-ow-ee-ow! Meeow! Meeow!"

The mouse stopped short at once. He looked round anxiously for the cat. But he couldn't see it anywhere.

"Meeow-ee-ow!" mewed the sailor doll, trying his hardest not to laugh. The mouse gave a squeal and looked at his cage. Dare he run right across the floor to it? Would the cat catch him as he went across? Well, he must try.

He scampered across the floor – and the sailor doll mewed again. The scared mouse turned aside and ran into the doll's house! The little front door was open, so he got in quite well.

"He's in the doll's house! Quick, shut the door!" yelled the bear. "You dolls in the doll's house, shut all the windows quick! Don't let that naughty mouse out!"

The curly-haired doll slammed the door of the house shut. The tiny dolls inside the house shut all the windows. Now the mouse was well and truly caught. He couldn't get out.

He went to a window and peeped out. "Where is that horrid cat?" he said, twitching his nose up and down very fast.

Nobody said a word. The mouse flew into a rage. "I don't

believe there ever was a cat! I didn't see one! I do believe it must have been one of *you* mewing, not the cat!"

The sailor doll giggled. He really couldn't help it. Then Bubble knew for certain that a trick had been played on him and he scampered up and down the little stairs in the doll's house, trying to get out. But he couldn't. What a furious rage he was in! He was so angry that he scared the little dolls and they had to get into the bedroom wardrobe to hide.

Then Alice and Ian came back into the playroom. They went to the mouse's cage and Alice gave a little scream.

"Oh no! The door of the cage is open! I do hope the mice haven't escaped."

Squeak was there, of course – but Bubble wasn't. So the two children began to hunt about all over the playroom. Alice was nearly in tears.

"He was so sweet. I did love him. Oh, Bubble, where have you gone?"

Bubble heard Alice's voice, and he pressed his little pink nose against a window in the doll's house, trying to see where Alice was – and quite suddenly, she saw him!

"Oh, look – isn't that Bubble in my doll's house? Yes, it is, it is – looking out of the window. Oh, Bubble, you look sweet in there. But you must come back to your nice cage at once."

Bubble was soon back in his cage, for Alice opened the front door of the doll's house, put in her hand and gently caught him. He was very glad indeed to be back in his nice, safe, cosy cage with Squeak.

The children looked at one another.

"You know," said Alice, "there's something strange about

this, Ian. I know the door and windows of my doll's house were open, because I opened them myself this morning. Well then – who shut them when Bubble got in? Whoever was it that caught him there?"

They looked round at the toys, sitting so still and quiet round the playroom. Alice looked hard at the sailor doll.

"He's got a wider smile than usual on his little face!" she said. "Sailor Doll, I'm sure you caught the mouse. Thank you very much. I shall let you go home with Ian to play with his toys as a reward."

So he did, and when the sailor doll came back he had quite a few stories to tell the other toys. It was a good reward for him, wasn't it?

Ho-Ho Plays
a Trick

THERE was great excitement in the Village of Bo. Old Mother Tippy's cottage had caught fire and had burned down to the ground. Mother Tippy had only been able to save two chairs and her bed, so the poor old dame was very sad and upset.

But the brownies of Bo came round and comforted her. "We will all give you what money we can spare!" they promised. "Then you will be able to get another cottage and buy what furniture you like!"

Ho-Ho said he would go round and collect money from every brownie in the village.

"But you won't get a penny piece from that mean old miser, Mister Snip-Snap!" said Gobo, grinning. "Nobody has ever known him to give any of his money away!"

"Well, I'll try, anyway," said Ho-Ho cheerfully. "He's rich enough to give me ten gold coins, goodness knows!"

Then off went the little brownie with a large collecting box, to get as much money as he could for old Mother Tippy.

When he came to the cottage where Mister Snip-Snap lived he heard a sound of angry shouting and he stopped. The brownie who lived next door poked his head out of the window, and called to Ho-Ho.

"Are you collecting money for Mother Tippy? Well, here is mine – but I warn you – don't go near Mister Snip-Snap today, whatever you do! He's in a most furious temper. Can't you hear him shouting?"

"Yes," said Ho-Ho, listening. "What's the matter with him?"

"You know that beautiful brooch he wears on the front of his jersey?" said the brownie. "It's a very magic brooch, and he thinks a great deal of it. Well, it's either lost or stolen! He looked down at his jersey this morning, and it wasn't there! He's hunted all through his house to find it and he can't, so he thinks a thief must have taken it."

"Well, I haven't taken it," said Ho-Ho. "I shall go and ask him to put something in my box for poor old Mother Tippy."

So, very bravely, he went up to the door of Snip-Snap's cottage and knocked loudly. The door flew open and there stood the old miser, his eyes gleaming fiercely, and his hair flying about all over his big head.

"What is it, what is it?" he snapped. "Have you brought me

news of my lost or stolen brooch?"

"No," said Ho-Ho. "I've come to ask you to give me some money to help poor Mother Tippy, whose cottage was burned down last night."

"Stuff and nonsense!" said Snip-Snap, rudely. "What do I care for that silly old woman? I'm much too busy this morning with my own troubles to bother about other people's. I never did like that old woman, anyway!"

"Don't be so unkind!" said Ho-Ho. "She is in great trouble. You are a mean old miser, Snip-Snap, and I hope you never find your brooch, so there!"

Snip-Snap was full of rage when he heard this. He lifted up his fist and struck out angrily at Ho-Ho. But the small brownie ducked his head, and Snip-Snap spun round in the air, and fell down in a heap on his front door mat. In a flash he jumped up and slammed the door in Ho-Ho's face.

Ho-Ho went down the path, grinning as he thought of how funny Snip-Snap had looked whirling and tumbling down on his mat. As he remembered this, he suddenly stopped and scratched his head. What was it that he had caught sight of on Snip-Snap's back as he fell? It was something bright and glittering!

Ho-Ho slapped his knee and laughed aloud. "Ho-ho-ho! Ha-ha-ha! Now I know what has happened to Snip-Snap's precious brooch! The silly fellow has put his jersey on back to front, so of course his brooch is at the back today, and he can't see it. Ho-ho-ho!"

Ho-ho laughed till the tears ran down his cheeks. Then he wiped them away and began to think. Couldn't he play a little trick on mean old Snip-Snap? Couldn't he somehow manage to get a lot of money out of him for Mother Tippy? He thought he could!

After a while he went back up the path to Snip-Snap's front door and knocked again, this time twice as loudly as before.

Snip-Snap put his head out of an upstairs window and roared: "Who is it now? What do you want? Go away!"

"Please, Snip-Snap, it's me again," said Ho-Ho.

Snip-Snap made a noise like a railway train going through a tunnel, and nearly fell out of the window with rage.

"Grrrr!" he roared. "I'll turn

you into a black beetle and tread on you, you nasty, twisty-toed little nuisance!"

"I may be nasty, but I'm not twisty-toed, Mister Snip-Snap!" said Ho-Ho, cheerfully. "I've only just come back to say that I know who's got your brooch. But if I'm a nuisance to you, I'll go. Good-bye!"

"Wait, wait!" yelled Snip-Snap, at once. "Tell me who has my brooch! The thief, the robber! Aha, wait till I get him, and I'll send him flying to the moon!"

"Oh, I wouldn't do that; you might be sorry!" said Ho-Ho, grinning.

"Nothing's too bad to do to the nasty person who has my precious brooch!" said Snip-Snap. "Quick, tell me!"

"I'll make a bargain with you, Snip-Snap," said Ho-Ho. "If I tell you who has your brooch and where it is, will you put ten gold coins into my collecting-box to give to old Mother Tippy?"

"You must be mad!" cried Snip-Snap. "Whoever would think of giving ten gold coins to that silly old woman!"

"Well, I would, for one, if I had them to give," said Ho-Ho. "But never mind, Snip-Snap – if you don't want to make a bargain with me, I'll go. I've a lot of collecting to do this morning."

Ho-Ho turned himself about as if he were going away. Snip-Snap gave a yell, slammed down the window and rushed down his stairs, four steps at a time. He flung open his front door and called to Ho-Ho.

"Stop! Stop! I'll give you five gold coins if you will tell me who has my magic brooch!"

"I said TEN!" said Ho-Ho, going down the path and opening the gate.

"Don't be silly," said Snip-Snap. "I can't possibly give ten."

"Well, of course, if your brooch

isn't worth ten gold coins, I can't expect you to give it," said Ho-Ho. "So I won't waste any more of my time or yours, Snip-Snap. Good morning!"

He slammed the gate shut. Snip-Snap tore down the path after him.

"I'll give you eight gold coins!" he cried.

"TEN!" roared Ho-Ho, who was thoroughly enjoying himself. He could see all the brownies who lived on either side, poking their heads out of their windows and grinning from ear to ear. What fun it was to play a trick on mean old Snip-Snap!

"Nine gold coins!" said Snip-Snap, in despair.

"TEN!" yelled Ho-Ho.

"Oh, very well", said Snip-Snap, sulkily, giving way suddenly. "I'll make it ten gold coins – but it's robbery, sheer robbery!"

"Not at all," said Ho-Ho, holding out his collecting-box, to Snip-Snap. "Not robbery at all – just a very generous gift from you to Mother Tippy – and very grateful she'll be, I'm sure!"

"I don't care tuppence about the old woman!" said Snip-Snap. "Here you are – one – two – three – four – five – six – seven –

eight – nine – ten – all pure gold! Now tell me who has my precious magic brooch and where it is! Stars and moons, won't I give that thief a nasty surprise!"

"I don't think I would if I were you!" said Ho-Ho, with a wide grin. "Thanks so much for your generous help. Now I'll tell you where your brooch is and who has it. Come here Snip-Snap!"

He took hold of the old miser and twisted him round. He undid the brooch from the back of his jersey and held it out to the astonished Snip-Snap with a polite bow.

"You had your brooch, and it was on your jersey as usual," he said. "But, dear Snip-Snap, you must have put your old jersey on back to front this morning. Good-bye, old fellow – and thanks again so very much for your ten gold coins for poor old Mother Tippy!"

Off skipped Ho-Ho, grinning all over his jolly little face, and the watching brownies roared with laughter to see the old miser, Snip-Snap, standing without a word to say, holding his precious brooch in his hand.

As for Mother Tippy, she was able to buy some beautiful new

furniture, and now she lives in a pretty little cottage as happy as can be – but what puzzles her very much is how Ho-Ho managed to get such a lot of money from old Snip-Snap the miser!

Really, it was very clever of Ho-Ho, wasn't it?

Good Dog, Tinker!

TINKER belonged to Robin and Mary. Sometimes he could be very good but at others he could be very naughty. It didn't seem to matter which he was, though, the children loved him just the same.

One day Robin gave Tinker a juicy bone to gnaw. "It's good for your teeth," he said. "And you've been such a good dog lately I think you really do deserve a bone!"

"Miaow!" said Sooty the cat. She liked bones, too, though she could only scrape them with her rough tongue – she couldn't manage to chew them.

Tinker looked at her, with the bone in his mouth. He dropped it for a moment and spoke to her.

"You can miaow all day if you like," he said. "But you won't get so much as one single sniff at this bone."

"Wherever you bury it I shall find it," said Sooty. She was very clever at finding where Tinker buried his bones, and he didn't like it. It was too bad to bury a half-chewed bone, and then, when next he came to dig it up to find that it wasn't there because Sooty had found it.

"I shan't bury it this time," said Tinker. "I shall hide it where you will never be able to find it!"

He trotted off with the bone. He took it into the dark tool shed, and lay down to chew it. It was a very hard bone and Tinker couldn't crunch it up. He had a lovely half-hour of chewing and gnawing. Then he heard Robin whistling for him.

"Walky, walky, Tinker!" called Robin, and Tinker knew he must put away his bone and go. But where should he put it? It must be somewhere clever, where Sooty would never find it. Tinker thought of all the garden beds in turn. No – Sooty would hunt in each one. Then he looked round the tool shed. Sooty never came in here! He would hide his bone somewhere here.

He was lying on a sack. What about tucking it inside the sack? Then no one would see it, and it would wait there for him to come back and chew it. That would be a fine hiding place.

So Tinker pushed his lovely, smelly bone into the sack, and then scampered off to join Robin and Mary.

He forgot about his bone till the evening. Then he wanted it again. Off he went to the tool shed to have a fine chew. But alas for poor Tinker, the door was shut fast! He stood and whined at it, he scraped it with his paw. But it was no use, the door wouldn't open.

"Bad luck, Tinker!" said Sooty nearby. "I suppose you've got your bone hidden in there! And you can't get at it. Dear, dear, what a pity to hide a bone in a silly place like that."

"Well, if I can't get it, you can't either," said Tinker with a growl, and ran off.

Now, the next day was a Sunday. The gardener did not come on Sundays, and so nobody went to open the tool shed to get out the tools. Poor old Tinker

ran to the shed a dozen times
that day, but he couldn't get in,
and he couldn't manage to make
Robin and Mary understand that
he wanted to have the door
opened.

So he had to go without his
bone. Sooty sat and laughed at
him, and when he ran at her in a
rage she jumped up on to the
bookcase and sat and laughed at
him there. She really was a most
annoying cat.

Now, that night somebody
went to the tool shed. It was
midnight and everyone in the
house was fast asleep. The
somebody was a robber. He had

come to steal as many tools as he could out of the shed!

He was very quiet, for he wore plimsolls. No one heard him, not even Tinker. He crept to the shed, and found it locked. But he guessed that the key was not very far away, and he soon found it, hung on a nail just under the roof of the shed.

He opened the door and slipped inside. He switched on his torch and looked round at the tools. They were very good ones, and the gardener kept them beautifully. The man grinned. Just what he wanted! He would be able to sell them for a lot of money. He took them down quickly from their nails and put them quietly together.

"I'd better slip them into a sack, in case anyone sees me on my way home," thought the robber. "I might meet the village policeman on his rounds." He looked about for a sack, and saw one on the ground. It was the one which Tinker had pushed his bone into. The bone was still there, very, very smelly now. The robber picked up the sack and shook it. The bone slid to the bottom and stayed there.

The man quietly put all the tools into the sack, and then put the bundle over his shoulder. It was terribly heavy. The robber went out of the door, locked it, and hung up the key again.

He went softly to the bottom of the garden. He put down the sack and squeezed through the hedge, pulling the sack after him. Then he put it on his shoulder again. He walked across the field with it, but it felt so heavy that he had to put it down on the ground again.

"I believe I could drag this sack behind me more easily than I could carry it," said the robber to himself. "It won't matter at all if it makes a bit of a noise now, because I am well away from any of the houses."

So he dragged the sack behind him over the field. He came to another hedge and squeezed through it. He went down a lane, still dragging the sack, and then, when he heard footsteps, he crouched down behind a bush, listening.

It was the village policeman. He had not seen or heard the thief, and he went slowly down the lane, thinking of the hot jug of cocoa that would be waiting for him when he got home.

The man crept out from his hiding place and carried on down

the lane. He came to the wood and slipped in among the dark trees. He made his way through the wood until he came to a big bank he knew where there were a lot of rabbit holes. He pushed the sack down a very big hole and pulled bracken and bramble sprays over the entrance.

"I'll come and get the tools when everyone has forgotten about them," he thought. Then off he went home.

Now, in the morning, Tinker ran to the tool shed early, for he knew the gardener would be there at seven o'clock to open the door. Sure enough, the man soon came along whistling. He took down the key and opened the door. Tinker darted in.

But the sack was gone – and his bone was gone! Tinker gave a howl of dismay – and at the same time the gardener gave a shout of surprise.

"Hey! What's happened to all my tools? They're gone!"

"Tools! Who cares about tools!" thought Tinker. "It's my bone that is really important. Oh, tails and whiskers, wherever can it be?"

The gardener went off to tell the children's father, and Tinker flew off to ask Sooty if she knew anything about his bone.

There was a great disturbance about the lost tools. The policeman was told and he came hurrying up to the house. Nobody paid any attention at all to poor Tinker and his lost bone. Sooty laughed at him.

"You needn't laugh!" said Tinker. "It was an important bone, and the robber stole that as well as the tools. I do wish I knew where it was."

"Well, go and sniff about and see," said Sooty, beginning to wash herself.

Tinker thought that was a good idea. He ran to the tool shed. Yes

– he could smell exactly where his bone had been, hidden in the sack in the corner. He ran out of the shed and began to sniff around the garden, hoping to get a smell of the bone somewhere.

When he came to the hedge at the bottom, he got very excited. There was the smell of bone there, quite distinctly. That was where the robber had put down the sack to squeeze through the hedge. The sack smelt strongly of bone and the smell had been left on the ground beneath the hedge. Tinker had a very sharp nose and he could easily smell it.

He squeezed through the

hedge. He ran into the field and sniffed about. He could smell nothing – till suddenly he came to the spot where the burglar had put his sack down and had begun to drag it behind him. The smell of bone was very strong there. With his nose to the ground Tinker followed it across the field, to the second hedge, through the hedge and out into the lane.

"Fancy the robber taking my bone with him in the sack such a long way!" thought Tinker. "It must have seemed a very fine and important bone to him. Now – here we go again – down the lane – behind this bush – down the lane again – and into the wood. Off we go – through the trees – to this bank – and oh, WHAT a strong smell of bone there is near this hole!"

Tinker scraped away at the rabbit hole, sniffing his bone all the time. It was in the sack of tools, pushed down the hole. Tinker couldn't get it out.

"I'll go back and get Robin and Mary to help me," he thought. So he trotted back in excitement, and by pulling at Mary's skirt and Robin's shorts, he managed to make them understand that he wanted them to follow him.

In great astonishment they went down the garden, through the hedge, across the field, through the second hedge, into the lane, and then into the wood to the big rabbit warren.

And there Tinker showed them the sack in the rabbit hole. "My bone's in there," he woofed to them. "Get it out, please."

But Robin and Mary were not at all interested in the bone – they shouted with joy to see the tools in the sack!

"Daddy's tools! Look, they're all here! Let's take them home this very minute. Won't Daddy be pleased? Oh, you very, very clever dog, Tinker, to find them for us!"

Tinker trotted home beside them, sniffing his bone eagerly. What a fuss there was when the children arrived home with all the tools!

They were emptied out and counted. Yes – they were all there! "Tinker, you shall have a very big, extra juicy bone today, for being so clever!" said Robin.

Well – that was good news. Robin rushed off to get the bone from the butcher's, and Tinker put his head inside the empty sack and dragged out his beautiful old bone as well!

"I must say you were terribly clever to find all of the things that were stolen by the robber," said Sooty, in a very admiring sort of tone. Tinker was extremely proud.

"Well – I am rather a clever dog, you see" he said, "and as you seem to have learnt that at last, I'll show you that I'm a very generous dog, too – you can have this bone, and I'll have the new one when it comes! And I say – have you heard? The policeman is going to hide in the wood till the robber comes to fetch the tools he hid. Then he'll be caught! I'm going to hide, too.

I shall have fun!"

Tinker did enjoy his bone – and Sooty enjoyed the other one, too. Wasn't it a good thing Tinker hid his first bone in the sack?

Its Nice to
Have a Friend

TIBS was the farm cat. She was a little tabby, with fine big whiskers and a nice long tail.

Punch was the farm dog. He was a big collie with a bushy tail and a very loud bark. He didn't like cats one little bit and Tibs didn't like dogs.

Tibs hardly ever went near Punch unless he was tied up, because she knew he would chase her, and Punch was always on the watch for her so that he might tear after her and send her flying up to the top of the wall, hissing and spitting. Then he would bark the place down!

Now, one day when Punch was

tied up he came out into the yard on his long chain to sniff at a roller that somebody had left there. He walked round it – and somehow or other his chain got twisted, and he couldn't get back to his kennel. There he was, held tightly by the roller, his chain pulling at his neck.

Punch pulled at it. He rolled over to try and get it loose – and all that happened was that he twisted his chain so much that it almost choked him!

He could only make a very little bark. He could hardly make a whine or a growl. So nobody heard him and nobody came to help him. He choked and struggled, but his chain was too tightly twisted round the heavy roller for him to get free.

Only Tibs, the farm cat, heard the noises he was making. She jumped on to the top of the wall and looked at poor Punch. What peculiar noises! What was the matter with him?

"Tibs!" croaked Punch. "Help me. I'm choking."

Tibs jumped down and had a look. No – she couldn't help him. She didn't know anything about chains! But she was sorry for Punch, and she thought of something else. She ran to the farmhouse and mewed loudly.

Mrs Straws, the farmer's wife, came to the door. "What is it?" she said. Tibs ran a little way away and looked back. The farmer's wife followed her – and then she, too, heard the strange noises that Punch was making out in the yard.

She went to see what they were – and in a minute or two she had undone the chain, untwisted it, patted poor Punch, and given him a long drink of water!

Punch looked at Tibs on the wall. "Thank you," he said. "You can come down and sit near me. I shall never chase you again.

You saved me from choking."

But Tibs didn't really trust him.
She would never come down
from the wall. Still, they had
many a talk together and that
was nice for both of them.

Then one day Tibs didn't come.
She didn't come for three days,
and then she told Punch why.

"I've got four little kittens,"
she told him proudly. "They're
my very own. They're in the
kitchen. But I do wish Bobby
and Betty, the children, would
leave them alone. They are
always pulling them about, and it
worries me."

The next day Tibs looked even

more worried. "Bobby took one of my kittens and dropped it," she said. "I'm going to take them away from the kitchen. I shall put them in the barn."

So she took each of her kittens by the neck and carried them one by one to a corner of the barn. But the children found them there and took them back to the kitchen again. They were like live toys to them, and they wanted to play with them!

Tibs was unhappy. She liked the children and she didn't want to scratch them. "But what am I to do, Punch?" she said. "One of my kittens has a bad leg because

Bobby squeezed it too hard yesterday. I wish I could think of somewhere else to take them."

Punch listened, his big head on one side. "I know a place where nobody would ever find them," he said. "But I don't think you'd like it. It's a place where nobody would ever, ever look."

"Where?" asked Tibs.

"In my kennel here!" said Punch. "There's plenty of good, warm straw – and plenty of room for you and your kittens at the back. I promise not to sit on you. I'll be very, very careful. You were good to me once – now let me be kind to you!"

Tibs thought about it. Did she trust Punch or didn't she? He was a dog. She was a cat. She didn't know if they could really be friends. Still – she would try!

So, when nobody was about, Tibs carried each of her kittens by its neck, all the way from the kitchen to the yard where the kennel was. One by one she laid the little things in the warm straw at the back. Then she settled down on them herself, purring happily.

Punch was very good. He didn't even let his tail rest on the kittens, and he gave them all the room he could. He even licked them when Tibs wasn't there, and when one of them patted his nose he was surprised and delighted.

The children looked all over the place for the kittens. They called and called Tibs. But she didn't come. She wasn't going to give her hiding-place away! Her kittens were safe and happy now. Punch sat in his kennel, so that nobody could even peep in. Aha! Look where you like, Bobby and Betty, you won't find the kittens!

"It's nice to have a friend," purred Tibs. "Nobody knows where I am. Keep my secret, Punch."

He will, of course – and we certainly won't tell it to Bobby and Betty, will we!

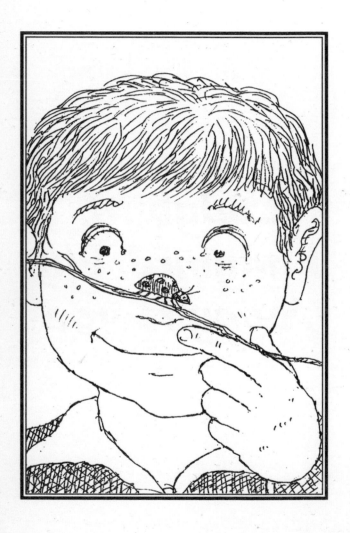

Ladybird, Ladybird, Fly Away Home

ONCE when Alistair was walking round his garden, he saw a big spider's web. He stopped to look at it – and as he watched, a little red ladybird, with pretty black spots on her back, flew straight into the web!

The web trembled – and out from under a nearby leaf rushed a big spider, hungry for a meal.

The ladybird struggled hard, but the web was sticky, and she could not free her feet or her wings. Alistair was sorry for her.

He took out a tiny stick and began to cut the web round the ladybird. The spider was frightened and went back to her hiding place, angry that her web was being spoilt.

"I'm sorry to spoil your beautiful web, spider, but I rather like ladybirds," said Alistair, and he took the tiny insect on to the end of his stick. The ladybird ran down the stick on to his finger.

She began to clean the web from her body. Alistair thought she was a dear little beetle. He watched her tuck her wings under her red wing cases, and then clean her legs thoroughly.

"I like you," he said. "I've done you a good turn, though I don't expect you know it. Hello,

Mother – look what I've just rescued from the spider – a little red ladybird with black spots on her back!"

"Nice little thing!" said Mother. "Well, you've done her a good turn. Maybe she will do us one some day!"

Alistair laughed. "Oh, she can't, Mother. We're so big and she's so little. Ladybird, ladybird, fly away home!"

The ladybird flew away – but she didn't fly far. She flew to Alistair's small garden. He had a rose tree there that he was very fond of – but oh, dear, it was covered with greenfly, and they

were eating the little new buds
and the leaves too.

The ladybird laid her eggs
there. Then she flew off again.
The eggs hatched out in a day or
two. From them came funny
little black beetles. They rushed
about, up and down the rose
tree, very lively indeed.

Alistair saw them one day.
"Mother, what are these little
black beetles?" he said. "Do you
see them on my rose tree? Oh
dear, what with greenfly and the
black beetles my poor tree will
soon be dead. I keep picking off
these greenfly but they come
again the next day. Shall I pick

off the new little beetles?"

"Oh no, Alistair!" said his mother. "Of course not. They are the children of the ladybird! She laid her eggs on your tree because she knew that there was greenfly food for them. Watch how they attack and eat the green blight!"

Sure enough, the little black beetles did eat the greenfly! They cleared stem after stem, leaf after leaf, and soon the tree was completely clear again. Alistair was glad.

"I suppose these beetles will one day turn into ladybirds themselves," he said. "Oh

Mother, I'm glad I rescued the ladybird! I did her a good turn – and now she has done me one too. I shall always put ladybirds on my rose trees when I find them, now!"

You can too, if you like. They will certainly be very good little friends to you!

The Mouse and the Snail

ALL summer long the fieldmouse had lived in his tiny little hole at the bottom of the sunny wall, and the snail had lived nearby.

At first they had taken no notice of one another at all, and then the mouse had begun to wonder why the snail always took his house with him wherever he went.

"Why don't you leave your shelly house behind when you go out?" he said. "It seems silly to have to drag it along with you all the time."

"It may seem silly to you, but it's perfectly sensible to me," said the snail. "I have a very soft body, and unless I wear my house over it, birds might fly down and peck me up at once. You see, I can't run away nearly as quickly as you can. I am a slow creature."

"Is your house heavy?" asked the mouse. "Can I come inside and have a look around?"

"Of course not. It just fits me," said the snail. "And no, it isn't a bit heavy."

"Shall we have a game?" asked the mouse, who was young and frisky and loved playing games. "Let's play hide-and-seek. You shut your eyes and I'll hide."

The snail rolled in his bigger pair of horns. "I'm hiding my eyes now!" he said. "My eyes are at the top of this pair of horns. I can pull them inside whenever I want to. Run and hide somewhere, little mouse."

The mouse thought they were strange eyes to have, but he was even more surprised to see the peculiar tongue that his new friend had. It was like a ribbon tongue, and it was set with thousands and thousands of tiny backward pointing teeth!

"Now you can see how it is that I manage to eat a whole lettuce leaf in a night!" said the snail.

"I use my tongue exactly like a file!"

The two became friends, though the mouse never liked going for walks with the snail, because he was so very slow in dragging his body along. Sometimes he left a bright, silvery trail, and the mouse thought that was pretty.

"I shall have to say goodbye to you now," said the snail, one autumn day. "I feel sleepy, I shall sleep for the whole winter."

"No, don't," said the mouse. "I stay awake throughout all of the winter and I shall want you to play with me. If you go to sleep I shall come and wake you up. I shall knock on your shell or I shall tickle you to make you wake up!"

But when he next went to play with his friend he couldn't wake him up at all! How could he tickle the snail's soft body? The snail had grown a hard little front door over the entrance to his shell, and the mouse couldn't reach it!

"He's not asleep! He's dead!" wept the mouse. "And he was so nice. He won't answer when I knock on his shell!"

But he wasn't dead, you know. He was only asleep. He will wake up and play with the mouse again in the warm springtime. He may be in your garden, so hunt for him and see his hard little front door!

The Tale of
the Tadpoles

THERE was once a small boy called Timmy. He went fishing one day in a little pond where some frogs had laid their eggs. They had laid them in jelly, but now, in the warm sunshine, the jelly had melted, and the eggs had hatched out into tiny little black tadpoles.

How they wriggled and raced round the pond! They were strange little things, all tail and head. Timmy wondered what they were. He put some in a jar and took them home, with some pondweed for them to cling to if they wanted to.

"Look, Mother!" he said.

"What are these? Haven't I got a lot of the little black wrigglers?"

"Yes, you have. Far too many," said his mother. "Now, Timmy, you like frogs, don't you – well, these tiny wrigglers will all change into frogs, if you take care of them properly. It will be like magic."

"Gracious! I'd like to watch them turning into frogs," said Timmy, who couldn't imagine how they did it. "But have I really got too many, Mother? I'd like a *lot* of frogs, you know."

"Well, if you do what most children do, and keep dozens in a small jar, they will all die, for there will not be enough air in the water for them all to breathe," said his mother. "Take all but five or six of them back to the pond, Timmy, and just keep those few."

So Timmy kept five in his jam-jar, and watched them carefully. Mother showed him how to tie a tiny bit of food on a string and hang it in the jar for them to nibble at. Then he pulled it out again so that it would not go bad, and make the water smelly and cloudy. He left the pondweed in because the tadpoles loved that.

One day he put them out in the jar in the sun. The hot sun

warmed the water, and soon the tadpoles rose to the top, turned over and looked as if they were dying. Timmy rushed to his mother at once.

"Oh, *Timmy*! They're slowly cooking in the sun poor things!" said his mother, whipping them away to a cool corner, and putting a little cold water into the jar. "Poor creatures! I hope they won't die. Hundreds of poor little tadpoles are cooked every year because children put them into the hot sun!"

"I didn't think," said Timmy, sadly. "I do hope they'll be all right, Mother. I do like them so very much."

They didn't die. They got better when they felt cool. So Timmy was able to watch the magic that turned the tadpoles, all heads and tails, into tiny frogs with four legs and a little squat body!

Their back legs grew, and then their front legs. Their tails became short. Timmy watched them each day, so he knew.

He gave them a cork to climb on, when they became tiny frogs, for now they liked to breathe the open air.

Then he put them into his garden so that they could find

new homes for themselves.

"Eat the grubs and flies for me," he said. "I've been a friend to you – now you can be a friend to me!"

Would *you* like to see frog magic too? Well, do as Timmy did, then, and keep a few tadpoles in a jar.